A Note to Parents and Caregivers:

Read-it! Readers are for children who are just starting on the amazing road to reading. These beautiful books support both the acquisition of reading skills and the love of books.

The RED LEVEL presents familiar topics using common words and repeating sentence patterns.

The BLUE LEVEL presents new ideas using a larger vocabulary and varied sentence structure.

The YELLOW LEVEL presents more challenging ideas, a broad vocabulary, and wide variety in sentence structure.

The GREEN LEVEL presents more complex ideas, an extended vocabulary range, and expanded language structures.

When sharing a book with your child, read in short stretches, pausing often to talk about the pictures. Have your child turn the pages and point to the pictures and familiar words. And be sure to reread favorite stories or parts of stories.

There is no right or wrong way to share books with children. Find time to read with your child, and pass on the legacy of literacy.

Adria F. Klein, Ph.D.
Professor Emeritus
California State University
San Bernardino, California

Managing Editors: Bob Temple, Catherine Neitge
Creative Director: Terri Foley
Editor: Jerry Ruff
Editorial Adviser: Mary Lindeen
Designer: Melissa Kes
Page production: Picture Window Books
The illustrations in this book were rendered digitally.

Picture Window Books
5115 Excelsior Boulevard
Suite 232
Minneapolis, MN 55416
877-845-8392
www.picturewindowbooks.com

Printed in the United States of America.

Library of Congress Cataloging-in-Publication Data
Blair, Eric.
Sleeping Beauty: a retelling of the Grimms' fairy tale / by Eric Blair; illustrated by
Todd Ouren.
p. cm. — (Read-it! readers fairy tales)
Summary: Enraged at not being invited to the princess's christening, a wicked fairy
casts a spell that dooms the princess to sleep for one hundred years.
ISBN 1-4048-0592-3 (reinforced library binding: alk. paper)
[1. Fairy tales. 2. Folklore—Germany.] I. Grimm, Jacob, 1785-1863. II. Grimm,
Wilhelm, 1786-1859. III. Ouren, Todd, ill. IV. Sleeping Beauty. English. V. Title.
VI. Series.
PZ8.B5688Sle 2004
398.2—dc22
2003028245

Sleeping Beauty

By Eric Blair
Illustrated by Todd Ouren

Special thanks to our advisers for their expertise:
Adria F. Klein, Ph.D.
Professor Emeritus, California State University
San Bernardino, California

Kathleen Baxter, M.A.
Former Coordinator of Children's Services
Anoka County (Minnesota) Library

Susan Kesselring, M.A.
Literacy Educator
Rosemount-Apple Valley-Eagan (Minnesota) School District

PICTURE WINDOW BOOKS
Minneapolis, Minnesota

Once upon a time, there lived a king and queen who had no children.

"Oh, how I wish we had a child," the king said to the queen.

Before a year had passed, the queen
had a lovely daughter. Everyone
called her Beauty.

The king gave a splendid party. He invited everyone he knew.

Twelve fairies came to the party. There were actually 13 fairies in the kingdom. One of the fairies was wicked, so she was not invited.

As the party came to an end, each of the 12 fairies gave Beauty a special gift. "You will be the most beautiful princess in the world," said one.

9

Another fairy came forward. "You will be the wittiest princess in the world," she said.

The fairies gave the princess
everything anyone could want.

After 11 fairies had given presents to Beauty, the bad fairy appeared. She was very angry because she had not been invited to the party.

The bad fairy put a spell on Beauty. "Here is my gift," she said. "When Beauty is 15 years old, she will prick her finger with a spindle and die." With that, the bad fairy left.

Everyone was frightened. But there was still one fairy who had not yet given a gift to Beauty.

"I cannot break the spell completely," the fairy said, "but Beauty will not die. She will sleep. After 100 years, a prince will come to wake her."

The king wanted to protect Beauty.
He ordered all the spindles in the
kingdom to be destroyed.

Beauty grew up with all the fairies' gifts. She was clever, pretty, sweet, and kind. Everyone loved her.

One day, when she was 15 years old, Beauty was alone in the palace. She wandered up the stairs of an old tower. At the top, she entered a room where an old woman sat spinning.

"What are you doing, dear lady?"
asked Beauty.

"I am spinning," said the old woman.

"Would you like to try?"

The old woman was really the bad
fairy. As soon as Beauty touched the
spindle, it pricked her finger, and she
fell into a deep sleep.

At that moment, sleep fell upon the whole palace. Knights, ladies, guards, footmen, pages, grooms, maids, and cooks all fell asleep. When the king and queen returned, they fell asleep, too.

A thorny hedge grew around the palace. It was impossible to enter. As time passed, many princes heard the story of Beauty and tried to get through the hedge. They all failed.

After 100 years had passed, another prince came into Beauty's kingdom. He heard an old man tell the story of the princess who slept in the palace behind the thorny hedge.

"I am not afraid," said the prince. "I will get through to wake the princess."

When the prince came near the thorny hedge, it magically became a hedge of beautiful flowers. It opened to let him enter. As soon as he had passed, the hedge turned back into thorns and closed behind him.

The prince came into the palace and found the sleeping king and queen.

He found the sleeping knights, ladies, guards, footmen, pages, grooms, maids, and cooks.

Finally, the prince came to the tower. He climbed the stairs and entered the room where Beauty lay.

The instant the prince saw Beauty, he
fell in love. He knelt at Beauty's side
and gently kissed her on her ruby
lips. At that moment, the spell was
broken.

Beauty awoke. She looked sweetly at the prince and said, "Is it you, my prince? I have been waiting for you for a very long time."

The rest of the palace woke up. The
thorny hedge disappeared. Beauty
and the prince were married that very
day and lived happily ever after.

Levels for *Read-it!* Readers

Read-it! Readers help children practice early reading
skills with brightly illustrated stories.

Red Level: Familiar topics with frequently used words and
repeating patterns.

Blue Level: New ideas with a larger vocabulary and a variety
of language structures.

Little Red Riding Hood by Maggie Moore
The Three Little Pigs by Maggie Moore

Yellow Level: Challenging ideas with an expanded vocabulary
and a wide variety of sentences.

Cinderella by Barrie Wade
Goldilocks and the Three Bears by Barrie Wade
Jack and the Beanstalk by Maggie Moore
The Three Billy Goats Gruff by Barrie Wade

Green Level: More complex ideas with an extended vocabulary
range and expanded language structures.

The Brave Little Tailor by Eric Blair
The Bremen Town Musicians by Eric Blair
The Emperor's New Clothes by Susan Blackaby
The Fisherman and His Wife by Eric Blair
The Frog Prince by Eric Blair
Hansel and Gretel by Eric Blair
The Little Mermaid by Susan Blackaby
The Princess and the Pea by Susan Blackaby
Puss in Boots by Eric Blair
Rumpelstiltskin by Eric Blair
The Shoemaker and His Elves by Eric Blair
Snow White by Eric Blair
Sleeping Beauty by Eric Blair
The Steadfast Tin Soldier by Susan Blackaby
Thumbelina by Susan Blackaby
Tom Thumb by Eric Blair
The Ugly Duckling by Susan Blackaby
The Wolf and the Seven Little Kids by Eric Blair

A complete list of *Read-it!* Readers is available on our Web site:
www.picturewindowbooks.com